Katherin
Thank you!

-Ellie

Thank you for
supporting chain-
free elephants
-Ellie

Foreword

When I was three years old I met my first elephants and their keepers and was in complete awe. However, I knew even then that something was terribly wrong.

My young friend, Ellison, also met her first elephants at a young age and knew, too, the grim reality in a short amount of time.

We both became attached to one elephant in Nepal; Samrat Gaj, a baby bull. Samrat lives chain-free with the other elephants at his home. He has toys and a kind caregiver. We now hope his story, told through the loving eyes of Ellison, will inspire more elephant lives to not only be saved, but savored.

We hope that Samrat and Ellison's journey continues to be one of light and love.

Blessings, dear Ellison, my fellow Elephant Warrior!

Your Friend,
Donna Marshall
Founder, Direct Aid Nepal

Ellie's Elephants

A true story of a little girl and her wish for chain-free elephants

Written & Illustrated by: Ellie Barnard

Illustrations by Ellie Barnard

ISBN-13: 978-1-0908-0245-3

Once there was a little girl,
named Ellie, who loved elephants.

LOVED elephants!

She got stuffed ones for
Christmas...

...she got balloons for her birthdays...

...and she'd even dress up as an elephant!

On any day, you could find Ellie playing with her toy elephants, or researching about them in one of her many books.

She had one giant stuffed elephant she'd take everywhere she went.

He still lives with her, eight years later.

Ellie and her family started traveling the world and seeing elephants **EVERYWHERE**.

Ellie loved her elephants.

Bali

Ellie met her first elephant in
Sri Lanka. It was AMAZING.
To her, being with the elephants was
a dream come true.

Sadly, Ellie later learned
that her beautiful
elephants weren't living
the life they should.

There were many
chained up elephants.

When Ellie saw them at
the river, bathing with their
caregivers, she saw CHAINS.

In Ellie's mind, there had to be a
better way to rescue elephants,
see them happy, and provide space
for them to be free.

But she was just learning...

Ellie and her family then visited
Thailand. They went to a place
where, sadly, they had a baby
elephant performing tricks.

Ellie was confused. The placed
called themselves "ethical".

She knew in her heart that this
was not nice, that the baby was
hurting, and this caused her heart to

BREAK.

Ellie's family visited another place in Thailand. Again, it seemed OK. Her favorite part was bathing them in the river and walking with them in the bush.

Ellie looked in the distance, and she saw people riding some of the elephants. For a moment, Ellie thought that would be **FUN**.

But then she felt badly that tourists, including people like herself, thought that elehant riding was OK to do.

She had learned it caused them pain...

...they had sores...

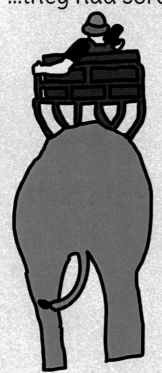

...and that the training was not nice.

They weren't treating the elephants with CARE and RESPECT.

Ellie's elephant journey
next brought her to Nepal.

While she was there, she met
two elephants, Srijana Kali,
and her son, Samrat,
who was only three months old.

They were wandering freely in
21 acres of fields by the river.

NO CHAINS.

An organization called
Direct Aid Nepal
helped build chain-free areas and
sun shelters, as well as provided
care for the elephants' caregivers.
So far, this was the best Ellie had
seen.

Srijana was rescued from the sad life of safari riding, as she wasn't wanted anymore. She was pregnant.

She wouldn't have to give rides to people anymore. People who didn't know any better.

She could just be an elephant.

While Ellie was there, she got to walk with the elephants to the river bank, learned how to make their food, called Kuchi, and fed them daily.

Ellie and baby Samrat spent **A LOT** of time together over the week.

She wished that **ALL** elephants could have a chain-free and ride-free life. She wished they were **FREE**.

Places like this are trying to keep elephants chain free and give them lots of SPACE.

Saving elephants means needing money for food, medicine, lots of land and providing for the caregivers.

Sadly, some places still offer elephant riding in return for money.

Like Ellie, people LOVE watching elephants, learning about them and they really want to see them happy.

It would be wonderful if tourists put their money towards seeing them roaming free in protected WILD reserves.

This could help save their habitats, while still protecting elephants.

Ellie left the lodge with Samrat, and all elephants, in her **HEART**.

Her mission now, is to help people make the most **ETHICAL** choices they can when visiting elephants.

Ellie is also supporting organizations looking to protect and care for rescued elephants like Samrat and his mom.

Organizations We LOVE

Direct Aid Nepal

Elephant Aid International

Bring the Elephant Home

B.L.E.S.

Thank you!

36317826R00018

Made in the USA
San Bernardino, CA
20 May 2019